Copyright © 2006 by NordSüd Verlag AG, Gossau Zürich, Switzerland
First published in Switzerland under the title *Timo und Matto wollen nicht das Gleiche*.
English translation copyright © 2006 by North-South Books Inc., New York.

All rights reserved. No part of this book may be reproduced or utilized in any form or by any means,
electronic or mechanical, including photocopying, recording, or any information storage and
retrieval system, without permission in writing from the publisher.

First published in the United States, Great Britain, Canada, Australia, and New Zealand in 2006
by North-South Books, an imprint of NordSüd Verlag AG, Gossau Zürich, Switzerland.
Distributed in the United States by North-South Books Inc., New York.

Library of Congress Cataloging-in-Publication Data is available.
A CIP catalogue record for this book is available from The British Library.

ISBN-13: 978-0-7358-2064-7
ISBN-10: 0-7358-2064-3
1 3 5 7 9 10 8 6 4 2

Printed in Belgium

Marcus Pfister

HOLEY MOLEY

Translated by J. Alison James

North-South Books

New York / London

Tim and Matt, two young mole brothers, were sitting together in a nice, grassy field. They were as different as night and day.

"Want to play something?" asked Matt.

"Playing is good," said Tim. "What should we play?"

"We could make something."

"Making something is good." Tim nodded.

"I've always wanted to make a hill," said Matt. "A really huge hill."

"Hills are no good," said Tim. "They're hot and high. I would much rather dig a hole. A really deep hole."

"A hole?" asked Matt. "We spend our entire lives underground, and finally when we have the chance to be outside, you want to turn around and dig a hole? That's the silliest thing I ever heard."

"Mama said that we have to dig a lot of holes to become big strong moles," Tim said defiantly.

"Mama said this, Mama said that . . ." Matt was getting annoyed. "You don't always do everything Mama says. If we build a hill, we could see over the tall grass and find out what else there is out there in the world."

"What else could there possibly be?" Tim said. "All you'd see is grass, grass, and more grass, and a lot of dirt from mole holes."

"You are so boring. You have absolutely no imagination," accused Matt.

"I am not boring!"

"Yes, you are!"

Then Tim shoved Matt, and Matt pushed Tim, and soon they were rolling on the ground.

"I don't want to play with you anymore," cried Tim and stamped furiously away.

"Who would want to play with you anyway?" Matt bellowed after him.

So Tim began to dig his own hole. It was no fun at all,
but at least Mama would be proud of his good work.

And Matt worked just as hard on his hill to show Tim that he could build a giant hill all by himself.

Matt longed to be high on his hill, looking out over the world. But even though he stood on the tips of his toes and craned his neck as far as it would stretch, his hill was still much too low. He simply could not see over the tall grass.

He decided to go take a peek at Tim's hole and see how he was coming along.

Tim was also curious. He slipped through the grass to spy on Matt. He wondered just how big his hill would be.

When Tim saw Matt's hill, he shook his head. There was something funny about this.

When Matt saw Tim's hole, he couldn't believe his eyes!

They had both built exactly the same thing.

By digging a hole, Tim had tossed up a pile of dirt, making a small hill.

By building up a hill, Matt had had to dig up dirt, leaving a small hole.

Matt was the first to snort with laughter.

Then Tim giggled, and they crawled out of their hiding places.

Once again, the two of them rolled on the ground—but this time they were laughing.

"That's what we get for fighting," giggled Matt. "If we'd worked together, then you would have had a deep hole, and I would have a huge hill!"

"We still can," said Tim. "Come on, let's go."